ARTHUR CHRISTMAS™

ARTHUR TO THE RESCUE!

Adapted by
ANNIE AUERBACH

STERLING CHILDREN'S BOOKS
New York

As the electronic present counter clicked down to zero on Christmas Eve, everyone at the North Pole headquarters gave a cheer. Santa, his son Steve, and all the elves had done it again. Another year, another successful Christmas present delivery!

But while everyone sat down for Christmas dinner, an elf named Bryony discovered that something had gone horribly wrong. A present was left behind. It was a bicycle for a girl named Gwen.

Steve said he couldn't deliver the gift. The new S-1 sleigh had to be repaired, and there just wasn't enough time before sunrise to get the present to Gwen.

A child without a gift on Christmas? Arthur, Santa's younger son, could not let that happen.

"She'll think she's the one kid Santa doesn't care about," he complained to Grandsanta. "She'll feel so left out."

Grandsanta had an idea. "Arthur, there is a way we can deliver Gwen's present!"

Grandsanta showed Arthur his pride and joy: Eve, his trusty old sleigh from when he was Santa. Grandsanta had kept Eve after Santa switched over to the new, fancy S-1.

Arthur couldn't believe his eyes. "The sleigh! The actual sleigh!"

Arthur wondered if the sleigh could still fly. Grandsanta grinned, his eyes twinkling, as he led Arthur through a large door.

Inside the room were eight reindeer.

"These are the great-great-grandchildren of the original eight reindeer," Grandsanta explained. "Dasher, Dancer, Prancer, er . . . Bambi? John?"

Grandsanta wasn't so good with names.

Arthur was overjoyed. "Oh, Grandsanta! You can get this present to Gwen. It's a miracle!"

"You're coming, too, lad," said Grandsanta.

"Me? On that? Up there? No way!" exclaimed Arthur. "I can't fly a sleigh. I can't even ride a bike without training wheels!"

Grandsanta wouldn't take no for an answer. "Ready?" he asked.

"NO!" cried Arthur, clinging to the side of the sleigh.

Grandsanta pulled a brass lever, and the reindeer were sprinkled with a sparkly cloud of magic dust. Up they went! They were on their way to England to find Gwen's house.

The sleigh flew across the sky. Grandsanta felt giddy. Arthur felt sick.

"We Clauses used to be the only men in the world who could fly," Grandsanta told Arthur. "It was a gift from Santa to his eldest son."

Now computers and elves did everything. The old traditions were gone.

Grandsanta was so busy talking that he forgot to watch where he was going.

"AHHHH!" they screamed.

They almost flew right into a skyscraper!

"I always come through Canada," shouted Grandsanta. "Nobody lives there."

They screamed again when an elf popped out of a hidden panel in the sleigh.

"Bryony Shelfley, Wrapping Operative Grade 3," the elf announced.

"A stowaway!" Grandsanta said with a scowl.

"There's a tear in your present's giftwrap," Bryony explained.
"I can wrap anything, sir, with three bits of sticky tape."
"Good," replied Grandsanta. "Wrap yourself a parachute."
Then he tossed her out of the sleigh!

Instantly, Bryony fired two tape guns at the sleigh. She hung by the tape until Arthur hauled her back in.

Bryony sat down and looked around.

"You've lost a reindeer," she pointed out.

It was true. One of the harnesses had broken. A reindeer had flown away. Where were they going to get a new reindeer now?

Grandsanta landed the sleigh near a tractor store. Arthur climbed a ladder to the roof where he struggled to take a big metal deer down.

"It's for Gwen," reminded Grandsanta. "'Eight beautiful reindeer.' That's what she's dreaming of. We're giving her the star treatment."

With eight reindeer leading the way once again, they flew on into the night. But they had no idea where they were going. They didn't have a GPS, and their map was VERY old.

Finally, Grandsanta spotted land. Unfortunately, it wasn't England, it was Africa.

Suddenly, they were surrounded by lions!

Grandsanta shouted, "They won't eat me. I'm Santa!"

Bryony jumped out like a ninja and yelled, "Only *children* get to tear the wrapping!" Then she taped a lion's paws together and gift-wrapped another lion's head.

They flew away from the lions, but when the group finally got to England, trouble found them again! The world military thought Eve was a UFO. They launched missiles at the sleigh!

Arthur and Bryony parachuted to the ground, using Grandsanta's original, red toy-sack. Meanwhile, Grandsanta took on the missiles.

BOOM! The sleigh exploded in the sky.

Grandsanta landed safely, while Arthur rode Gwen's bicycle through the town to her house. Bryony wrapped it on the way. They didn't have much time. It was almost dawn. They had to get the present to Gwen before she woke up!

Arthur made it just in time. He placed the bike under the Christmas tree and watched Gwen open the present. Her face glowed with excitement.

The S-1 came to pick up Arthur, Grandsanta, and Bryony. They had accomplished their mission. Every child had received a present.

Arthur had saved Christmas!

Behind the Scenes

The amazing art and dynamic animation for *Arthur Christmas* was not made overnight. It took artists years to perfect every last detail of the characters and environments. Before making it to the big screen, the talented teams at Aardman Animations and Sony Pictures Animation created hundreds of character and location sketches, sculptures, and paintings for inspiration. Their CG (computer-generated) experts then took that hand-drawn artwork and used it as a basis for the final film you see in theaters. Here is some "behind-the-scenes" art that shows how *Arthur Christmas* came to life!

Final painting and developmental sculpture of Grandsanta

Painting of animals floating above Africa

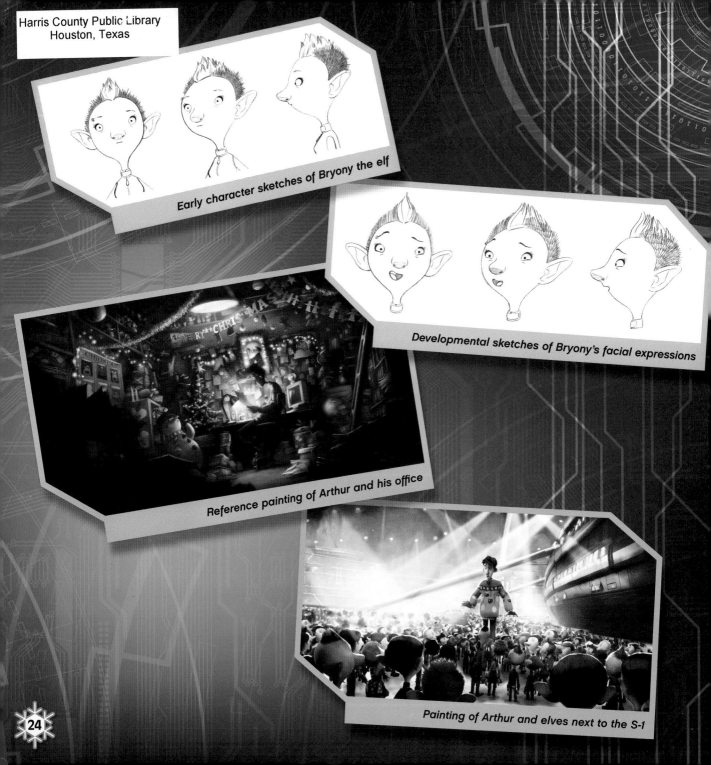

Early character sketches of Bryony the elf

Developmental sketches of Bryony's facial expressions

Reference painting of Arthur and his office

Painting of Arthur and elves next to the S-1

24